I0672851

The Memory Keeper's Apprentice

P. A. Farrell

Copyright ©2025 by Patricia A. Farrell, Ph.D. All rights reserved. No part of this book may be used or reproduced in any form or by any means or stored in a database or retrieval system without the prior written permission of the author, except in the case of brief quotations embodied in critical articles and reviews. Making copies of any part of this book for any purpose other than your own personal use is a violation of United States copyright laws. The author does not recognize "fair use" distribution to classes, seminars or any other form of training or information provided to other individuals, institutions or other potential users of this information. For information on rights and permissions requests, address them to Dr. Patricia A. Farrell, Patricia A. Farrell, Ph.D., PO Box 761, Tenafly, NJ 07670.

This book is sold as is, without warranty of any kind, either express or implied, respecting the contents of this book, including but not limited to implied warranties for the book's quality, performance, merchantability, or fitness for any particular purpose. Neither the author nor dealers or distributors shall be liable to the purchaser or any other person or entity with respect to any liability, loss, or damage caused or alleged to have been caused directly or indirectly by this book.

Cover photo: PaulFleet@istockphoto.com

The Pocket Companion Series contains:

When Your Mind Won't Stop

After the Loss: Finding Your Way Through Grief

You Are Enough: Rebuilding Your Self-Worth

At the Crossroads: Making Decisions When Nothing Feels Clear

When People Hurt: Navigating Difficult Relationships

When You Feel Stuck: Finding Movement in Hard Times

Books by Patricia A. Farrell, Ph.D.

When You Can't Pour From an Empty Glass: CBT Skills for Exhausted Caregivers

The Little Book on Learning Big Critical Thinking Skills

The Smart Kid's Survival Guide: Making Good Choices in a Confusing World

How to Be Your Own Therapist

P. A. FARRELL

It's Not All in Your Head: Anxiety, Depression, Mood Swings and Multiple Sclerosis

Unfiltered: Beneath the noise of our thoughts lies the true narrative of our minds

Unfiltered Again: A behind-the-scenes look at healthcare, medicine and mental health

A Social Security Disability Psychological Claims Handbook: A simple guide to understanding your SSD claim for psychological impairments and unraveling the maze of decision-making

A Social Security Disability Psychological Claims Guidebook for Children's Benefits

The Disability Accessible US Parks in All 50 States: A Comprehensive Guide

Birding in the US NOW!: A birding guide for individuals with disabilities

Contents

Chapter One: The Sign in the Window

The pawn shop sat wedged between a store that sold things for under a dollar, a bedraggled and closed-down hardware store, and the laundromat that no one seemed to use. It was here that Riley Bennett had learned to keep his eyes down and his pace quick.

A bone-chilling wind swept through downtown, carrying wood smoke from someone's stove and warning of an early snow. Tightening his jacket and slowly reading the handwritten sign taped inside the shop's window, "Help wanted, serious inquiries only," he decided to take a chance. After all, he needed a job, and this seemed like a place he could find one.

Three months since he dropped out of college. Two months since his landlord started leaving increasingly pointed notes about back rent. One week since the collection agency began calling about his mother's medical bills, the ones he'd co-signed for when he was eighteen and full of hope. The bills had outlived her by fourteen months now, growing interest like mold in a forgotten basement.

Riley pressed his palm against the shop's glass door, took a deep breath, and decided he had to do this. His reflection stared back at him—twenty-two years old and already carrying the exhaustion of someone who had learned that working two jobs still wasn't enough. No, it was nowhere near enough to cover his responsibilities and bills. Beneath his hand, the glass felt unnaturally cold, cold enough that he almost pulled away. It didn't make sense. But rent was due in six days, and the gas station had just cut his hours again. He was out of options. This had to work. He needed another job.

The shop's interior looked like every other pawn shop Riley had ever been desperate enough to enter. Guitars hung on the far wall, their strings probably loose and their cases long gone to other transactions. A jewelry counter ran along the right side, filled with engagement rings that someone had decided weren't worth keeping, even an assortment of wedding bands. Sports equipment cluttered one corner—baseball bats, a hockey stick with tape still wound around its handle, a basketball that had lost most of its air. But something felt off about this place, something that made Riley's skin prickle even before he noticed the absence of price tags on any of the items. No price tags? Did that mean this guy would try to soak somebody for every cent they had? Yeah, that's probably what he did. At least Riley thought that might be what he was doing.

Behind the counter sat a man who looked like he had been carved from the same weathered wood as the shop itself. His hair had turned gray in a way that suggested it was once dark, and his hands rested flat on the counter with the calm patience of someone who knew how to wait. When he looked up at Riley, his eyes were pale blue and seemed to see right through whatever confidence Riley was trying to put out.

"The sign said you're hiring," Riley said. His voice came out rougher than he'd intended, scraped raw from the cold walk downtown.

The man didn't respond immediately. Instead, he studied Riley with an intensity that made Riley want to check if his shirt was buttoned wrong or if something embarrassing was written across his forehead. The silence stretched between them like taffy, pulling thinner and thinner until Riley was certain the man would simply tell him to leave. He waited for the man to say something, anything.

"Warren Kemp," the man finally said. He didn't offer his hand to shake. "You ever worked in a pawn shop before?" This was a guy who was very direct and his question showed it.

"No, but I've been in enough of them." Riley tried for honesty, figuring lies would be transparent to someone with eyes like that. "I need work. I'm reliable, I show up on time, and I don't steal." There it was all out on the table, and he waited for the response.

Warren's mouth twitched at one corner, not quite a smile. "Those are baseline requirements for being human, not qualifications for employment." He stood up from his stool, and Riley realized the man was shorter than he'd expected, maybe five-foot-seven, but he carried himself with the weight of someone much larger. "What I need is someone who can keep their mouth shut and their judgments in check. Someone who understands that other people's stories aren't entertainment." This was an odd beginning to a job interview.

Riley thought about his mother's hospital room, the way visitors had whispered in the hallway about how young she was, how sad it all was, turning her dying into a narrative they could consume and feel moved by. He thought about the collection calls, the way the woman on the phone spoke about his debt like it was a moral failing rather than a mathematical inevitability.

"I can do that," Riley said. This was the truth because he had kept his mouth shut on many occasions when he wanted to scream something and hadn't.

Warren moved around the counter with surprising grace for someone his age—Riley guessed somewhere in his early sixties, though something about the man suggested he might be older or younger, existing in a space where age became irrelevant. He walked to the shop's front window and flipped the OPEN sign to CLOSED, even though it was only two-thirty in the afternoon. Why was he closing the shop now? Riley couldn't figure that one out.

"This isn't a regular pawn shop," Warren said, his back still to Riley. "We don't deal in objects, not really. We deal in memories." Memories? Weren't pawn shops where you took valuables to exchange them for money? How could you buy a memory?

Riley waited for the punchline, the moment when Warren would crack a smile and admit he was messing with the desperate kid who'd walked in looking for work. But when Warren turned around his expression held nothing but absolute seriousness. This guy meant business.

"Memories," Riley repeated, tasting the word. An explanation would be appropriate now Riley thought.

"Memories," Warren confirmed. He gestured around the shop. "Everything you see here—the guitars, the jewelry, the sporting equipment—these are just anchors. Physical objects that held meaning for someone. But what we actually trade in, what people actually bring us, are the memories attached to those objects."

Riley's first instinct was to walk out. His second instinct was to laugh. His third instinct, the one that actually took hold, was to stay very still and listen, because Warren Kemp didn't look like a man who made jokes or wasted time on elaborate pranks. This was the time for Riley to keep quiet.

"How does that work?" Riley asked.

Warren moved to one of the guitars on the wall, a battered acoustic with a crack running through its body. He touched it with the reverence most people reserved for religious artifacts. "A man brought this in six months ago. Tommy Vickers worked at the plant for thirty years before it closed. He brought the guitar and the memory of his daughter's wedding, the first dance he had with her before she moved to Seattle and stopped calling. He said the memory hurt too much to keep."

"And you... what? You took it?" He knew the question was pretty dumb because the man already said he took it because it was hanging on the wall. But there was a story attached to that guitar.

"I store it," Warren said. "Along with the guitar. And when the time is right, when Tommy's ready, he can come back and reclaim it. Or someone else can experience it if they need to understand something about loss or love or letting go."

Riley's head felt too full, too crowded with impossibilities trying to wedge themselves into the space where his understanding of reality had been comfortably sitting. "That's not possible."

"Isn't it?" Warren's pale eyes fixed on Riley again. "Close your eyes."

"What?" Riley's concern now was that something was about to happen, and he wasn't sure he wanted to participate.

"Close your eyes. Think about a memory that matters to you. Something specific. Not just a general feeling or an idea, but an actual moment you can step back into."

Riley wanted to refuse, wanted to walk out of the shop and forget this conversation ever happened. But his feet stayed planted on the worn floorboards, and his eyelids grew heavy. He thought about his mother's kitchen, the yellow wallpaper with tiny sunflowers that she'd always meant to replace but never got around to. He could smell the coffee she'd brew too strong, could feel the texture of the Formica countertop beneath his palms, could hear the exact sound of her laugh when he'd said something that surprised her into joy.

When he opened his eyes, Warren was nodding. "You went somewhere just now. I could see it on your face. That's where the memories live—in those spaces between heartbeats, where the past feels more real than the present. I just help people store them somewhere safer than their own heads."

Riley swallowed. His throat felt tight. "And you want to hire me to do what, exactly?" He wasn't sure he could do it or if he wanted this job, but desperation was stronger than anything.

"Learn," Warren said simply. "Watch. Listen. Help people when they come in carrying something too heavy to hold onto. And most importantly, help me keep watch for the ones who've figured out what we do here. The ones who want to take these memories for themselves."

"Who would want that?" It almost sounded like people were thieves who wanted to steal memories, and that he had to watch so they didn't.

Warren's expression shifted, and for the first time, Riley saw something that looked like fear flicker across the older man's features. "There are things in this world that feed on pain, on regret, on the moments people wish they could forget. This shop protects those memories, keeps them from being consumed. If you work here, you'll be part of that protection. You'll be a keeper."

The shop seemed to grow colder around them, and Riley couldn't tell if it was his imagination or something else, something that made the guitars on the wall tremble slightly on their hooks.

"When do I start?" Riley heard himself say it, surprise by how much he meant it. He didn't even ask what he would be paid for his work. And the deal was done.

Chapter Two: The First Transaction

R iley's first week at the Memory Keeper's shop passed in a blur of inventory counts and cleaning jobs that kept him busy but away from the shop's real business. He dusted the jewelry counter, reorganized the sports equipment, and tuned the guitars, even though Warren said they'd be out of tune again by morning. The older man watched him work closely, like Riley's old shop teacher who waited for students to make mistakes before stepping in.

On the eighth day, a woman walked into the shop carrying a shoebox. Things had been slow and she was the first customer he'd seen since he started in the shop.

She looked about forty-five, her body showing signs of weight changes that had stretched her skin. Her hair was pulled back in a limp ponytail, streaked with gray she didn't try to cover. But Riley noticed her eyes most of all: red-rimmed and hollow, as if all meaning had been drained out, leaving only the act of seeing.

Warren came out of the back room when the bell over the door chimed. He walked to the counter with the same calm grace Riley had seen when they first met. The woman's shoulders dropped a little, as if just seeing him let her relax.

"Brenda," Warren said. Not a question, just an acknowledgment.

"I can't keep it anymore, Warren." Her voice scraped out, raw and used up. "I thought I could. I thought I was supposed to. But I can't."

Warren nodded slowly. "Show me."

Brenda put the shoebox on the counter. Her hands trembled as she opened it, and Riley moved closer, forgetting Warren's earlier advice to keep his distance. Inside was a child's baseball glove, small enough for a six- or seven-year-old, with the name KEVIN written in marker on the thumb.

The air in the shop shifted. Riley first felt a tightness in his chest that made it hard to breathe. Then a pressure built behind his eyes, like the start of a migraine. The temperature dropped so fast that his breath turned visible. What was happening must have been expected by Warren.

Warren placed his hand flat on the counter, inches from the shoebox. "Tell me what you're bringing."

"The day I found him," Brenda said. Her words came faster now, like she needed to expel them before they poisoned her from the inside. "The day I came home from work early and found Kevin in the bathroom. The tile was so cold. I'd always meant to put down a bath mat, something warmer, but I never got around to it. And his skin was cold too, and I knew, I already knew, but I still called his name anyway. I still shook him like maybe he was just sleeping on the bathroom floor at three in the afternoon."

Riley's stomach turned. He wanted to ask her to stop, to cover his ears like a child afraid of scary stories. But Warren's face stayed calm and kind, not pitying, so Riley made himself stay silent, too.

"He'd been struggling," Brenda continued. "Depression, anxiety, all the things they tell you to watch for. But he was only twelve. Twelve. How does someone that young decide they're done?" She pressed her palm against the shoebox lid. "I've carried this for four years. The memory of finding him, the cold tile, the way his baseball glove was sitting on the sink counter like he'd meant to put it away but got distracted. I wake up every morning and it's the first thing I think about. It's worn grooves in my brain, Warren. Deep grooves I can't climb out of."

Warren reached across the counter and put his hand over hers. The gesture was simple, almost fatherly, but Riley saw something pass between them, a silent understanding that went deeper than words.

"You don't have to carry this alone anymore," Warren said. "But you need to understand what you're asking. If I take this memory, if I store it here, it won't be gone from you completely. You'll still know it happened. You'll still remember Kevin. But the sharpness will dull. The way it cuts you every morning will soften. Do you understand?" As he spoke he looked into her eyes with a kindness Riley had rarely seen before.

Brenda nodded, tears tracking down her face. "I just want to re-member the good parts again. I want to remember his laugh, the way he'd throw himself into things he loved. I can't reach those memories anymore. This one's blocking everything else."

"Alright," Warren said. He looked over at Riley. "Come here." The command was unexpected and Riley wasn't sure what he was sup-posed to do now but he approached Warren.

Riley's legs felt numb, but he managed to walk to the counter. Up close, he saw Brenda's hands were covered in small scars, the kind you get from years of work in a kitchen or factory. Her fingernails were bitten down to the quick.

"Put your hand here," Warren instructed, pointing to a spot on the counter next to the shoebox. "Not on the glove itself. Just on the counter."

Riley did as he was told, and as soon as his palm touched the wood, he felt it. Something cold and electric ran through the surface, up his arm, into his chest, and settled behind his ribs.

Warren placed his other hand on top of Riley's. "Feel that?"

"Yes," Riley managed. Something surreal was happening and he didn't want to question and he knew he needed to participate.

"That's the memory. It's looking for a new place, somewhere other than Brenda's mind. We're going to give it a new home." Warren's voice grew softer and steady, almost like a prayer. "Brenda, hold the glove. Think about that day. Don't push it away. Let yourself feel it all, just once more." It was almost hypnotic what was happening.

Brenda picked up the baseball glove with shaking hands and pressed it to her chest. Her face crumpled. The sound she made was not quite a sob or a scream, but something deeper, like the sound of a wound being sealed. Was that possible?

The shop got colder. Frost appeared on the inside of the windows. Riley's hand under Warren's started to burn with that electric current, now stronger and pulsing like a heartbeat. He felt something moving through him, images that weren't his: a bathroom with blue tile, a small still body, a mother's scream that never really faded.

"Now," Warren said, and he pressed Riley's hand harder against the counter. "Release it, Brenda. Let it go into the wood, into the building, into the space we've made for it. You don't have to hold it anymore."

Brenda's grip on the glove loosened incrementally. The current running through Riley intensified until he thought his skin might split open from the pressure. Then, all at once, it stopped. The cold vanished. The pressure released. Riley gasped and pulled his hand back, staring at his palm like it might have changed somehow.

Brenda slumped against the counter, but her face looked different. The emptiness in her eyes had faded a little, as if someone had finally turned up a light that had been dim for years.

"It's done," Warren said gently. "The glove stays here. The memory stays here. You can visit whenever you need to, whenever you're ready to hold it again for a little while. But it won't follow you home anymore."

Brenda nodded, wiping at her face with the back of her hand. She looked at Riley then, really looked at him, and something like recognition passed across her features. "You're new."

"Yeah," Riley said. His voice came out hoarse.

"It's hard at first," she said. "Feeling other people's pain. But Warren will teach you how to hold it without letting it overwhelm you." She stood up straighter, and Riley saw she looked lighter, as if a weight had been lifted. "Thank you," she said as she looked at Warren. Then, to Riley: "Thank you for helping." He could still feel a trace of that current, that transfer of something too heavy for one person to carry alone.

"What did we just do?" Riley asked.

Warren picked up the baseball glove carefully and carried it to a shelf behind the counter. He set it next to other items: a wedding ring, a pocket watch, a child's stuffed rabbit. Each one seemed to hold its own meaning.

"We gave her permission to keep living," Warren said. "Sometimes that's all people need—to let go of the moments that are crushing them." He turned to Riley. "You felt it, didn't you? The memory moving through you?"

"I saw..." Riley struggled for words. "I saw pieces. The bathroom. Her son. God, he was so young."

"The memories aren't just kept here, Riley. They exist somewhere between the physical and the emotional, between what happened and what it meant. You'll learn to move through that space. You'll learn to carry some of other people's pain so they don't have to carry it all alone." Warren looked Riley in the eye. "Can you do that? Because once you start, once you open yourself to these memories, you can't go back to not knowing. You can't go back to thinking the world is simpler than it is."

Riley thought about his mother's hospital room, the medical bills, and all the small humiliations of being young, broke, and weighed down by debt. But he also remembered Brenda's face, how the emptiness had faded, and how she left the shop standing taller.

"I can do it," Riley said.

Warren smiled, a real smile that reached his eyes. "Good. Because tomorrow, someone will come in with something even heavier. And you'll help me make sure it doesn't destroy them."

Chapter Three: The Soldier's Burden

Travis Holbrook showed up at the shop on a Tuesday morning, and Riley could tell right away that something was off. Warren's whole body tensed when Travis walked in, and the older man's hand went to his chest, as if making sure his heart was still beating. Riley was just starting to understand that these were signs of danger.

Travis was maybe thirty, built like someone who'd spent years training their body into a weapon. He wore civilian clothes, jeans and a flannel shirt, but he moved like a soldier, all economy and purpose. His eyes scanned the shop with the awareness of someone who'd learned to catalog exits and potential threats before allowing themselves to relax. Those eyes were dark brown, almost black, and they carried weight that Riley recognized from Brenda but multiplied, concentrated into something that looked almost toxic.

"Warren," Travis said. His voice came out flat, carefully controlled.

"Travis." Warren moved around the counter, but slower than he had with Brenda, like he was approaching something that might detonate. "How long have you been back?"

"Three months." Travis's jaw worked, muscles jumping beneath his skin. "Three months of trying to convince myself I could handle it. Trying to convince Jennifer that I was fine, that I just needed time." He reached into his jacket pocket and pulled out a small object wrapped in camouflage cloth. "I can't do it anymore. I can't keep pretending the memories don't own me."

Riley stayed behind the counter, following Warren's earlier instruction to observe unless specifically called forward. But his attention fixed completely on Travis, on the way the man's hands shook as he unwrapped the cloth to uncover a set of dog tags.

The temperature in the shop dropped so quickly that Riley's teeth hurt. Frost spread across the windows again, but this time it made geometric patterns, as if someone was drawing with ice. The guitars on the wall gave off a low hum that Riley could feel in his bones.

Warren's face had gone pale. "Travis, what memory are you bringing?"

"Kabul," Travis said. The word fell into the space between them like a stone into still water, creating ripples that spread outward. "The checkpoint. The day Mitchell died. The day I should have died."

Riley's stomach clenched. He'd read the news, seen the headlines about the withdrawal from Afghanistan, about the bombing at the airport. But reading about something and standing five feet from someone who'd lived through it were entirely different experiences. He knew he was about to hear something upsetting.

"That's a heavy memory," Warren said carefully. "One of the heaviest you could bring. Are you sure you want to release it?"

"I'm not releasing it," Travis said. His voice cracked on the words. "I'm trying not to let it kill me. I wake up at three a.m., and I'm back there, Warren. I'm back at that checkpoint and I'm watching Mitchell walk toward the crowd and I'm yelling at him to stop, to wait, but he doesn't hear me or he doesn't care or maybe he knows what's about to happen and he's trying to save the rest of us."

Travis's hands clenched around the dog tags. "I'm watching him die on repeat. Every night. Every time I close my eyes. Every time a car backfires or someone slams a door. I'm there, and I can't leave, and Jennifer keeps saying I need to talk to someone but how do I explain that talking doesn't stop the replay? How do I explain that my brain is a broken projector showing the same scene forever?"

Warren glanced at Riley, then back at Travis. "If I take this memory, it won't erase your guilt. You understand that, right? You'll still know what happened. You'll still carry responsibility for surviving when Mitchell didn't."

"I know," Travis said. "I'm not trying to forget. I'm trying to learn how to remember without it destroying me." He held out the dog tags. "Please."

Warren took a breath so deep his entire chest expanded. He nodded once, then gestured for Riley to come forward. "We'll need both of us for this. Military memories, especially trauma this fresh, they fight being stored. They want to keep replaying because that's what trauma does—it convinces your brain that if you just watch it enough times, you'll find a way to change the outcome."

Riley moved to Warren's side. His legs felt unsteady, like he'd been running for miles. When he looked at Travis, he saw the man's eyes were wet, tears tracking down his face that he made no attempt to wipe away.

"Both hands on the counter," Warren instructed Riley. "This is going to hurt. These kinds of memories, they don't want to leave. They're going to cling to Travis and they're going to try to cling to you, because they're looking for anyone who'll carry them."

Riley put both hands flat on the worn wood. The electric current he'd felt with Brenda's memory started right away, but this time it was sharper and more aggressive, like touching a live wire. His breath caught in his chest.

Warren put his hands over Riley's. "Travis, hold the dog tags. Tell us what happened. Don't spare any details. The memory needs to fully emerge before we can store it."

Travis's hands shook as he lifted the dog tags. His voice came out ragged. "It was August twenty-sixth. One hundred degrees and we could barely breathe through the dust and the crowd. There were so many people trying to get to the airport, trying to get out before the Taliban took complete control. Mitchell and I were working the checkpoint, trying to process people fast enough to keep the crowd from turning into a stampede."

The current running through Riley's hands grew stronger. Images flickered at the edges of his vision: heat rising from the concrete, faces pressed against barriers, and the sharp smell of sweat and fear.

"There was this woman," Travis continued. His voice had gone monotone, detached, like he was reading a report rather than reliving the worst day of his life. "She kept screaming that her baby was sick, that she needed to get through. Mitchell said he'd check it out, make sure the baby was okay. I told him to wait, to let someone else handle it, but he was already moving into the crowd."

Riley's vision filled with the memory now, like watching a movie projected directly onto his retinas. He saw Mitchell—tall, dark-haired, maybe twenty-five—pushing through the crowd toward a woman in a burqa. He saw Travis yelling, his mouth forming words Riley couldn't hear. He saw Mitchell reach the woman, saw him lean down to look at the bundle she was holding, saw the exact moment Mitchell's face changed as he realized it wasn't a baby.

The explosion ripped through Riley's mind as if it were happening to him. The sound hit first, so loud it wiped out all thought and turned everything into pure noise. Then came the heat, the pressure, and the feeling of being thrown back. When things came back into focus, Riley saw through Travis's eyes: what was left of Mitchell, the crater in the concrete, and bodies scattered like toys.

Riley screamed. Or maybe Travis screamed. Or maybe they both did, voices merging in shared agony as the memory fought to consume them both.

Warren's hands pressed harder on Riley's. "Hold it," Warren commanded. "Don't let it take you. You're here, in Millbrook, in this shop. You're safe. The memory belongs to Travis but you're just a conduit. Let it flow through you, not into you."

Riley couldn't breathe. His lungs had forgotten their function. The smell of burning filled his nose—burning fabric, burning flesh, burning everything. His ears rang with the aftermath of the explosion, and beneath that ringing he could hear Travis's voice, hoarse from screaming Mitchell's name over and over.

"Release it," Warren said to Travis. "Give it to the shop. Give it to the building. Let it live here instead of in your head."

Travis's entire body shook. The dog tags swayed in his grip, catching the dim light from the shop's overhead fixtures. His mouth moved, forming words: "I'm sorry, I'm sorry, I'm sorry."

The current through Riley reached a crescendo. For one terrible moment, he thought his heart might stop, thought the memory might be too much for a human body to process. Then Warren did something—Riley couldn't see what, couldn't understand the mechanism—but the pressure released all at once. The current cut off. The images vanished. Riley found himself gasping, bent over the counter, his palms aching like they'd been burned.

Travis crumpled. He didn't fall completely, just sort of folded in on himself, his back hitting the shop's front door with a thud. His face was wet with tears and sweat, his chest heaving with sobs that sounded like they'd been locked away for months.

Warren moved around the counter with surprising speed. He knelt beside Travis, one hand on the younger man's shoulder, and said something too quiet for Riley to hear. Travis nodded, still sobbing, and handed over the dog tags.

Riley straightened slowly, every muscle in his body screaming. He watched Warren place the dog tags on a shelf with the same reverence he'd shown Brenda's baseball glove. The tags settled into place, and Riley could have sworn he heard them still humming, still vibrating with the weight of what they carried.

"Oh, my God," Riley whispered.

Warren returned to the counter. His face had aged a decade in the last ten minutes, lines deepening around his eyes and mouth. "That," he said quietly, "is what we're protecting people from. That's what we keep safe here."

Riley looked at Travis, who was slowly pushing himself to standing. The hollowness in his eyes hadn't completely filled in the way Brenda's had, but something had shifted. He could see Travis breathing more easily, his chest rising and falling with less desperation.

"It's still there," Travis said, his voice rough. "In my head. I can still remember it."

"You'll always remember it," Warren said gently. "But now it's not living in your body the same way. Now you can remember without reliving. There's a difference, even if it's hard to feel that difference right now."

Travis nodded and looked at Riley. There was a moment of understanding between them, a shared sense of what Riley had just experienced and carried. "Thank you," Travis said. Then he left the shop, moving more slowly than before but standing straighter, as if he had finally set down a burden that had thrown him off balance.

Once the door closed, Riley and Warren stood in silence. Riley's hands kept shaking. His head felt packed with images that weren't his, sounds he'd never really heard, and smells he'd never actually known.

"That was what you meant," Riley said. "When you said there are things that feed on pain."

Warren nodded. "Memories like that, trauma that intense, they have energy. A flavor. And there are entities in this world that can taste that flavor, that hunt for it." He looked at Riley with those pale blue eyes. "That's why this shop exists. That's why we do what we do. We take the memories that are killing people, and we store them somewhere safe, somewhere protected. Because if we don't, those entities will find them. They'll consume them. And they'll consume the people carrying them."

Riley thought he should be scared. Thought he should walk out right now and never come back. But instead, he found himself asking, "What do these entities look like?"

Warren's expression darkened. "That's a conversation for another day. For now, you need to go home, get some rest. Eat something. Drink water. You just carried part of someone's worst memory through your body. That takes a toll, even on experienced keepers."

Riley nodded, but his feet didn't move toward the door. He looked around the shop—at the guitars, the jewelry, the sports equipment, all the anchors for memories too heavy for single individuals to carry. "How many are stored here?"

"Hundreds," Warren said. "Maybe thousands. I stopped counting years ago." He walked to the window and looked out at Third Street, at the normal world going about its normal business. "Every item in this shop represents someone's pain, someone's joy, someone's regret. They're all here, waiting. Some people come back to reclaim their memories once they're strong enough. Some never do. And some," his voice dropped, "some memories get claimed by things that have no right to them."

"Has that happened before?"

Warren didn't answer. But the silence was answer enough.

Chapter Four:
The Third Street Shadows

For the next three days, Riley moved through life as if underwater. Everything seemed muffled and far away, haunted by Travis's memory that lingered in his mind. He burned his eggs at breakfast, distracted by flashes of Mitchell's face before the explosion. He almost crashed his car leaving the gas station when a door slammed, his body reacting like a bomb had gone off. At night, he lay in his bed in his apartment, listening to sirens, traffic, and his neighbors arguing through thin walls. None of it felt as real as what had happened in Warren's shop.

On the fourth day, Riley returned to work even though Warren had told him to take the week off. His apartment felt too small, too quiet, too full of his own thoughts. At least in the shop, he could occupy himself with dusting and reorganizing and pretending that the items around him were just items, nothing more. He needed distractions and he knew going to the shop would provide them.

Warren looked up from behind the counter when Riley walked in. The older man's face showed neither surprise nor disapproval, just a kind of weary understanding. "Couldn't stay away?"

"I needed to see it again," Riley said. "The shop. The memories. I needed to know it was real and not just... I don't know. A breakdown. Exhaustion. Something explainable."

Warren gestured around the shop. "It's real. All of it. The good news is you'll get used to it. The bad news is you'll get used to it."

Riley moved to the counter, his hands finding the same spot where he'd placed them when helping with Travis's memory. The wood still felt cold beneath his palms and still hummed with that electric current. "Do you feel them? The memories? All the time?"

"Every minute of every day," Warren said. "But I've learned to live with it. Learned to let them flow around me instead of through me. You'll learn that too, if you stay long enough."

"How long have you been doing this?"

Warren's mouth twitched. "Longer than you'd believe. This shop, or versions of it, has existed in Millbrook for generations. I inherited it from the previous keeper, who inherited it from the keeper before that. The building itself is special—built on a convergence point, a place where the barrier between the physical and emotional world grows thin. That's what allows us to store memories the way we do."

Riley looked around the shop differently now. He used to think it was just old, worn down by years of people coming and going. But now he noticed other things: shadows gathered in corners where sunlight should reach, the air felt heavier near some shelves, and time seemed to shift depending on where you stood.

"What happens if someone breaks in?" Riley asked. "If someone tries to take the memories?"

Warren's expression darkened. "That's what I've been trying to pre-vent for the last forty years. There are protections on this building, wards that keep most entities out. But nothing's perfect. Nothing lasts forever. And recently..." He trailed off, his gaze moving to the shop's back room, to a door Riley hadn't been allowed to enter yet.

"Recently what?" Tension was getting to him and he needed to know what he should be expecting.

Before Warren could answer, the shop's phone rang. The sound was jarring in the quiet space, shrill and insistent. Warren picked up the receiver, listened for a moment, and his face went pale.

"When?" Warren asked. Then: "How many?" A pause. "I'll be there in ten minutes."

He hung up and immediately started moving, grabbing his coat from behind the counter, checking his pockets for keys. "Riley, I need you to watch the shop. Don't let anyone in. Don't let anyone touch anything. And whatever you do, don't go into the back room. I'll explain when I get back."

"What's happening?"

Warren paused at the door, his hand on the handle. "Someone tried to break into Sheila Morrison's house last night. She's one of our clients, brought in a memory six months ago. Whoever broke in didn't take anything valuable—no electronics, no jewelry, nothing. They just ransacked her bedroom, tore apart her closet, destroyed photos. They were looking for something."

Riley's stomach dropped. "The memory she brought here?"

"Probably. Which means someone knows what we do here. Some-one knows what we store." Warren's pale eyes met Riley's. "Lock the door behind me. Don't open it for anyone you don't recognize. I'll be back soon."

After Warren left, Riley locked the door and turned the sign to CLOSED. The empty shop felt different—bigger somehow, with deeper shadows and the weight of all those memories pressing down on him. He walked through the space slowly, seeing each item in a new way. The wedding ring belonged to someone. The child's stuffed rabbit belonged to someone. The baseball glove, the dog tags, the pocket watch—each was a piece of a life, a moment too painful or too precious to carry alone.

Riley found himself drawn to Travis's dog tags. He didn't touch them, but he stood close enough to feel the residual energy radiating from the metal. He could almost hear the echo of the explosion, almost smell the burning, almost feel the heat. The memory wasn't stored in his brain anymore, but his body remembered. His body would always remember.

A sound from the back room made Riley freeze.

It was soft, barely more than a whisper—a sliding sound, like something being dragged across the floor. Riley's heart started to race. Warren had told him not to go into the back room, but he had also left Riley alone in a shop full of stored trauma, with only a vague warning that something might try to feed on them.

Riley moved toward the back room door. His hand hovered over the doorknob, and he could feel cold air seeping out from underneath, could smell something that reminded him of ozone and old metal. The doorknob felt ice cold beneath his palm.

"Don't," a voice said behind him.

Riley spun around, his heart pounding. A woman stood by the shop's front window, even though he was sure the door was still locked and he would have heard someone come in. She looked about sixty, dressed in old-fashioned clothes: a long skirt, a high-collared blouse, and her hair pulled back in a tight bun. But it was her eyes that unsettled him. They were too pale, almost colorless, and they never blinked.

"The back room isn't for you," the woman said. Her voice sounded wrong, layered, like multiple people speaking in unison. "Not yet. Not until you understand what you're protecting."

"Who are you?" Riley managed. His voice came out strangled. "How did you get in here?"

The woman smiled, and Riley noticed her teeth were too white, too perfect, too uniform. "I've been here longer than Warren. Longer than this building. Longer than this town. I've been here since the first person in Millbrook felt regret deep enough to scar their soul."

She came closer, and Riley saw that she didn't really walk—she seemed to glide, her feet barely touching the floor. The air grew colder with every step she took. "The memories in this shop are delicious," she said. "Each one a feast of pain and loss and guilt. I can taste them from outside these walls. I can feel them calling to me. But Warren's protections keep me from taking what I want."

Riley backed up until his spine hit the counter. "You're what he was talking about. You're the thing that feeds on memories."

"One of many," the woman said. Her colorless eyes fixed on Riley with predatory focus. "There are dozens of us in Millbrook, hundreds across the Midwest, thousands across the world. We go where pain concentrates, where trauma pools. Usually, we feed on the living, on people too broken to protect themselves. But Warren's shop offers something special. Concentrated pain. Refined trauma. Memories so potent they could sustain us for years."

"You can't have them," Riley said. The words came out more confident than he felt. If he was going to protect the shop as Warren had indicated he should it was now.

The woman laughed, and the sound was like wind through a grave-yard. "I don't need your permission, little keeper. Warren's protections are weakening. I can feel the cracks forming. Soon, I'll be able to walk through these walls and take what I want. And there's nothing a dropout college kid with debt problems can do to stop me."

She vanished.

She didn't walk away or leave through the door. She simply van-ished from where she stood, leaving behind only the smell of ozone and a cold spot in the air that made Riley's breath show.

Riley's legs gave out, and he slid down the counter to sit on the floor. His heart pounded so hard he thought he might be sick. His hands shook. Every part of him wanted to run, to leave the shop and never return, to forget about Warren Kemp, memory keeping, and the things that fed on pain.

But he thought about Brenda and her son's baseball glove. About Travis and his survivor's guilt. About all the people who'd brought their worst moments here and trusted Warren to keep them safe. If Riley left now, if he abandoned this place, what would happen to those memories? What would happen to the people who'd given them up?

Warren found Riley still sitting on the floor twenty minutes later. The older man took one look at Riley's face, at the frost still lingering in the air, and his expression shifted into something grim.

"She was here," Warren said. Not a question. He knew, and he knew who it had been.

"A woman. Old-fashioned clothes. Colorless eyes. She said—" Ri-ley's voice cracked. "She said the protections are weakening."

Warren closed his eyes and leaned heavily against the counter. For the first time since Riley had met him, the older man looked genuinely old, genuinely tired. "Her name is Vera. Or that's what she calls herself.

She's been trying to get into this shop for forty years. Every keeper has to face her eventually."

"What does she want?"

"Everything," Warren said. "All the memories. All the pain. She wants to consume every moment of suffering stored in this building because that's what she is—pure hunger given form. She exists to feed on regret and guilt and trauma." He looked down at Riley. "I should have warned you better. Should have explained what you'd be up against. But I needed help, and you were willing, and I told myself you'd learn as you went."

Riley pushed himself to standing. His legs felt steadier now, the initial shock wearing off. "Teach me," he said. "Whatever you know about protecting this place, about keeping the memories safe. Teach me." There was no doubt that Riley had just had an interaction that required Warren give him more training and do it right now.

Warren studied Riley's face for a long moment. Then he nodded. "Alright. But first, you need to understand exactly what we're dealing with. Come with me."

He led Riley to the back room door.

Chapter Five: The Archive

The back room shouldn't have existed. Riley knew the shop's size from the outside. It was maybe twelve hundred square feet, a narrow rectangle squeezed between two other buildings. But when Warren opened the door and motioned for Riley to follow, Riley stepped into a space that made no physical sense.

The room stretched back much farther than seemed possible, with walls lined by shelves that disappeared into shadows the lights couldn't reach. Each shelf held hundreds of items. Some looked like things from the front shop, while others were completely unfamiliar. Riley spotted a child's shoe, a pair of reading glasses, a kitchen timer, and a gardening trowel. Each item gave off the same electric feeling Riley had noticed with Brenda's baseball glove and Travis's dog tags, but here it was stronger, layered, a mix of pain, joy, and regret that made his head spin.

"This is the Archive," Warren said. His voice echoed strangely in the vast space, bouncing off walls that shouldn't exist. "Every memory brought to this shop for the last hundred and fifty years is stored here.

Some items have been reclaimed by their owners. Some never will be. Some have been here so long I've forgotten whose pain they contain."

Riley walked slowly down the center aisle, his head tilted back to take in the impossible height of the shelves. "How is this possible?"

"The building wants to protect the memories," Warren said. "So it's bigger on the inside than the outside. Space changes here. Physics doesn't always apply. Don't try to make sense of it. You'll just end up frustrated."

Near the back of the Archive, Riley noticed a section where the items looked older—antique pocket watches, bonnets, and spectacles with wire frames. "How far back do these go?"

"The shop was established in 1873," Warren said. "Right after the railroad came through Millbrook. The town grew fast; people flooded in looking for work and opportunity. With growth came trauma—industrial accidents, disease, domestic violence, and all the ways people hurt each other and themselves. The first keeper recognized that some people's memories were destroying them, and they needed a place to lay down their burdens. He touched one of the older items, a woman's hair comb. "This belonged to Catherine Hillman. She brought the memory of her daughter's death from cholera. She visited this shop every week for thirty years, holding the comb, remembering her child without being destroyed by the grief. When she died, she left instructions for the comb to stay here, so her daughter would be remembered by someone."

Riley felt the weight of responsibility settle on his shoulders. They weren't just storing memories. They were becoming guardians of the dead, holding onto moments that would otherwise disappear. It was a physical memory trove that should have been impossible but existed here.

"Warren," Riley said carefully, "what happens when you die? Who takes over?"

Warren's expression shifted, and for a moment Riley saw genuine fear in the older man's eyes. "That's the problem. Keeping takes a toll. The memories wear on you, age you faster than normal. Most keepers last maybe twenty or thirty years before the weight becomes too much. I've been doing this for forty, and I can feel myself running out of time." He looked at Riley. "I don't have an heir. No children, no family. I'd been searching for someone I could train, someone who could take over when I'm gone. And then you walked through that door, desperate enough to take a job you didn't understand."

"You're dying," Riley said. Not a question.

"Slowly," Warren admitted. "But yes. Maybe I have a year left. Maybe two if I'm lucky. Which means I have that long to teach you everything you need to know about running this shop, about protecting the memories, about fighting off entities like Vera." He gestured around the Archive. "This is your inheritance now, whether you wanted it or not. These memories are your responsibility."

Riley's breathing grew shallow. The reality hit him hard: he had only a year or two to learn an impossible job, to protect hundreds of people from things that fed on their pain, and to guard a building that broke the rules of nature. He thought about leaving, about saying no to this overwhelming responsibility. He'd never signed up for something like this. It was just supposed to be a simple job.

But then he remembered his mother's hospital room and the weight of her death he carried each day. If someone had given him a place to set down that memory, to visit it only when he was ready instead of being crushed by it every morning, he would have accepted. Who wouldn't? In that instant he knew what he had to do.

"Okay," Riley said. "Teach me."

Warren smiled, and relief flooded his features. "First lesson: the protections. Come with me."

They walked to the far end of the Archive, where the shadows deepened and the air had a metallic taste. Warren pulled back a curtain Riley hadn't seen before, revealing a wall covered in symbols. Some looked a bit like Nordic writing, while others were completely unfamiliar. The symbols were carved into the wood and filled with something that looked like silver.

"These are wards," Warren explained. "Protection sigils that keep entities like Vera from entering the building and consuming the memories. They were put in place by the first keeper and maintained by every keeper since. But they require regular renewal, regular feeding." He looked at Riley. "They feed on the keeper's life force. A little bit each time, not enough to kill but enough to age you, to wear you down."

"That's why you're dying," Riley said. "You've been feeding these wards for forty years."

"Exactly. And Vera knows it. She can feel the wards weakening because I'm weakening. That's why she's getting bolder, why she was able to manifest in the shop today. She's testing the boundaries, looking for cracks." Warren traced one of the symbols with his finger. "I need to renew them tonight. And you need to watch, to learn, because soon you'll be doing it yourself."

They spent the next hour as Warren explained each symbol, what it protected against, and how to feed it with his life force. Riley tried to remember the patterns, but the symbols seemed to change when he looked away, shifting just enough to make memorizing them impossible. The effort was incredibly tiring.

As evening approached, Warren prepared for the renewal. He lit candles around the Archive's perimeter, creating a circle of flickering light that pushed back the shadows. Then he stood before the wall of symbols, placed both palms flat against the wood, and closed his eyes.

Riley watched Warren's face twist in pain. The symbols started to glow, silver light pulsing with Warren's heartbeat. The older man gasped for breath, his whole body shaking. Riley saw him age right in front of him: new lines appeared on his face, his hair turned whiter, and his shoulders slumped under an unseen burden.

Then Riley felt it—a pull in his chest, as if something was trying to draw his life toward the wall. He stumbled back, breaking the connection, and the feeling stopped. But Warren kept going, giving more of himself to the wards, making them stronger even as it aged him. He was protecting the shop from Vera with his very life.

When Warren finally pulled his hands away, he looked ten years older. His face had gone gray, his hands trembling. He sagged against the wall, breathing hard.

"My God," Riley whispered. "Warren—"

"It's necessary," Warren said, his voice rough. "If I don't renew them, the wards fail. If the wards fail, Vera gets in. If Vera gets in, every memory in this building gets consumed, and every person who trusted us to keep them safe gets destroyed." He looked at Riley with eyes that suddenly seemed ancient. "This is what it means to be a keeper. This is the price." It was also, he knew, the price Riley would have to pay if he took over the shop after his apprenticeship.

Riley helped Warren back to the front shop. Warren moved as if he were decades older than he had been that morning. They sat quietly for a long time, Warren catching his breath while Riley tried to make sense of what he'd seen.

"I can't do that," Riley finally said. "I can't pour my life into those wards and age myself to death." After what he'd seen, Riley wasn't sure this was an apprenticeship he could handle adequately.

"You won't have to," Warren said. "Not for a while yet. The renewal I just did should hold for another month, maybe six weeks. And I'll teach you techniques to minimize the cost, to draw strength from the memories themselves rather than just from your own life force. It's not perfect, but it extends how long a keeper can survive." He looked at Riley. "I've lasted forty years because I learned those techniques. Most keepers burn out in twenty because they don't." There was a way he might be able to do it, Riley thought, and perhaps he could.

"What happens if there's no keeper?" Riley asked. "If I say no, if I walk away, what happens to the memories?"

Warren's expression grew bleak. "The wards fail within weeks. The entities move in and consume everything. The people who brought their memories here get overwhelmed by them again, but this time worse because the memories come back corrupted, twisted, weaponized. Some might survive. Most won't. Millbrook would see a spike in suicides, overdoses, violent outbursts—all the ways that unprocessed trauma manifests when it has nowhere else to go." The prospects of what might happen if he were to refuse this job shocked Riley. He couldn't leave people to those fates if he were able to do something.

Riley thought about Brenda, imagined her waking up one morning with her son's death flooding back into her consciousness at full strength. He thought about Travis, imagined the explosion replaying in his head with renewed intensity until it drove him to desperate action. He thought about all the other people whose memories filled this building, all the pain that Warren had been protecting for four decades.

"I'll do it," Riley said. "I'll learn. I'll become the next keeper." The bargain was sealed.

Warren reached out and gripped Riley's shoulder. His hand felt frail, bones sharp beneath thin skin. "Thank you," he said. "I know this isn't what you signed up for. But you're saving lives by agreeing to this. Saving more lives than you can imagine."

That night, Riley walked home through Millbrook's quiet streets. The town looked the same as always: small, ordinary, a bit run-down, full of people just trying to get by. But now Riley saw it differently. He noticed the burdens people carried, the memories that weighed them down. He sensed the darkness at the edges, the things that fed on pain waiting nearby.

He also noticed the light in windows, the laughter from bars, and the small moments of joy that helped people get through hard times. For the first time, he realized that his work at the Memory Keeper's shop was about protecting those good moments as much as storing the painful ones. Without a safe place to put down their burdens, people couldn't make space for happiness. They couldn't heal or keep going.

Riley climbed the stairs to his apartment, unlocked the door, and stood in the doorway looking at his small, worn-out space. A month ago, it had felt like a prison, a reminder of what he'd lost and what he couldn't have. But tonight it felt different. It felt like home—imperfect and temporary, but his. Tomorrow, he would return to the shop to keep learning how to protect memories, fight off things that fed on pain, and become a keeper.

That responsibility should have scared him. Instead, it felt almost like having a purpose.

Chapter Six: The Consumed

Riley discovered Colleen Brennan's body on a Thursday morning.

He got to the shop early, before Warren, hoping for some quiet time with the memories in the Archive. He had been practicing what Warren called "resonance," the skill of sensing a memory without touching its anchor object. This meant feeling the emotional weight of stored moments from afar. It would help him figure out which memories needed more protection, which ones were becoming unstable, and which ones were attracting entities like Vera.

The shop's front door was unlocked. That struck Riley as odd because he knew the shop was always secured each evening.

Riley's stomach tightened right away. Warren always locked the door when he left and checked it twice. If the door was open, it meant someone had broken in, the wards had failed or been bypassed, and the memories were at risk.

Riley pushed the door open slowly. The shop looked untouched: guitars hung on their hooks, jewelry sat in its case, and sports equipment was stacked in the corner. But the temperature felt off, colder than it should be for November, and the air smelled like ozone mixed with something rotten and organic.

Then Riley saw her.

Colleen Brennan was crumpled near the counter, her body twisted in a way that made Riley feel sick. Her eyes were open, staring at nothing, and her mouth was frozen in a scream. But her chest was what made Riley stumble back. It looked hollowed out and collapsed, as if something had reached inside and taken everything important.

Riley's hands shook as he took out his phone. He knew he should call 911, get the police and an ambulance, and follow the rules. But something held him back. Some instinct told him that calling the authorities would only make things worse and bring attention the shop couldn't handle.

Instead, Riley called Warren.

"Get here now," Riley said when Warren answered. His voice came out strangled. "Someone's dead. Colleen Brennan. She's in the shop."

Warren arrived within minutes. He took one look at Colleen's body and his face went ashen. "Vera," he said. "Or one of her kind. They didn't just kill her. They consumed her memories first, then her life force."

"We need to call the police," Riley said. But even as the words left his mouth, he knew they sounded wrong. This wasn't something the police could handle. This wasn't something that could be explained in official reports.

Warren knelt beside Colleen's body, his hand hovering over her collapsed chest. "Colleen brought a memory here three weeks ago. Her daughter's overdose. She'd found the girl in her bedroom, needle still in her arm, pupils dilated. It was destroying Colleen, that image. She couldn't sleep, couldn't eat. She came here desperate." Warren's voice cracked. "I told her the memory would be safe. I promised her."

Riley looked around the shop, searching for signs of forced entry, signs of how Vera had gotten past the wards. But everything looked intact. "How did she get in?"

"She didn't," Warren said slowly. His eyes settled on something behind the counter, a small object Riley hadn't seen before. It was a compact mirror, tarnished silver with an ornate pattern on the back. "Colleen brought that with her daughter's memory. The mirror was what the girl used to cook the heroin, to heat the spoon before injection." Warren's face twisted as he realized his mistake. "I stored it wrong. I put it in the front shop instead of the Archive. It wasn't protected by the full wards." Now Riley knew that there was a hierarchy for storing memories.

"So Vera could access it?"

"She couldn't come into the shop directly, but she could send part of herself through an unprotected object. She used the mirror as a doorway." Warren stood up and walked over to the compact mirror. Riley noticed his hands shaking as he picked it up. As soon as Warren touched the silver, frost spread across its surface. "The memory's gone. Vera consumed it. And then she consumed Colleen." There was no mention of how Colleen could have entered the shop or how the door had been opened without being unlocked. Riley decided to let those two things go for now.

Riley felt sick. He'd been learning to protect memories for less than two weeks, and already someone was dead because of a keeper's mistake. "What do we do with her body? We can't just leave her here."

Warren pulled out his phone with the careful movements of someone whose hands weren't quite steady. He dialed a number and spoke quietly into the receiver. "Kent, it's Warren. I need your help. Yes, another one. She's at the shop. Twenty minutes? Good."

After Warren hung up, Riley asked, "Who's Kent?"

"Millbrook's county coroner. He knows a little about what we do here. Not everything, but enough to realize some deaths in this town are unusual. He'll call this natural causes, probably heart failure, and document it so the family can have closure." Warren looked down at Colleen's body, and Riley could see the guilt on his face. "This is my fault. I got careless, rushed the storage, didn't follow protocol. And now Colleen's dead."

They waited in silence for the coroner to arrive. Riley couldn't stop looking at Colleen's face, at the terror frozen in her features, at the way her body had been hollowed out from the inside. This was what happened when keepers failed. This was the cost of mistakes.

Kent arrived driving an unmarked van. He was maybe fifty, built solid like someone who'd spent years lifting bodies, with a face that suggested he'd seen too much death to be shocked by it anymore. He took one look at Colleen and his jaw tightened. "How many does this make, Warren?"

"Four in the last six months," Warren said quietly.

"They're getting bolder." Kent knelt beside the body and examined Colleen with a professional calm. "Same marks as the others: collapsed chest cavity, life force extraction, memory consumption. Whatever you're fighting, it's winning."

Riley felt cold spread through his limbs. Four deaths in six months. Four people who'd trusted Warren to protect their memories and paid for that trust with their lives. "Why didn't you tell me people were dying?" He knew he was indicting Warren for a shortcoming, but he also knew that Warren was becoming weaker and Vera knew that.

"Because if I'd told you, you never would have taken the job," Warren said. His voice carried an edge of defensiveness. "And I needed help. I needed someone I could train before I ran out of time completely."

"You should have been honest."

"Maybe." Warren's shoulders slumped. "But would honesty have changed anything? Would knowing that keepers fail, that people die, that entities like Vera are winning have made you better prepared? Or would it just have scared you away?"

Riley wanted to be angry, wanted to feel betrayed. But looking at Warren's face, at the exhaustion and guilt etched into every line, he found he couldn't summon the energy. Warren was right. If Riley had known the full scope of what he was signing up for, he probably would have walked away. And then Warren would be facing this alone, would be dying alone, and even more people would lose their memories to entities that fed on pain.

Kent placed Colleen's body into his van with practiced efficiency. Before he left, he looked at Riley. "You're the new keeper?"

"I guess so," Riley said.

"Good luck," Kent said. His tone made it clear Riley would need it. "And Warren, you need to tell the community about the failures. People deserve to know their memories might not be safe here."

"If I tell them, they'll stop coming," Warren said. "Then where will they go with their pain? Will they go back to suffering alone? Will we see the suicide rates we had before this shop opened?"

Kent didn't have an answer for that. He drove away with Colleen's body, leaving Riley and Warren alone in the shop.

"I need to move the compact mirror to the Archive," Warren said. "Need to put it somewhere Vera can't use it as a doorway. And I need to check every other object in the front shop, make sure I didn't make the same mistake anywhere else." Whatever was in the front of the shop needed to be evaluated for its possible use as a gateway for Vera.

They spent the rest of the day checking every item in the front shop for weaknesses and moving anything risky to the Archive's protected shelves. With each object Riley touched, he felt the weight of stored memories. There was so much pain, so much trauma, and so many people trusting that their worst moments would be safe here. The weight of his apprenticeship became apparent as he touched every item.

By evening, Riley's hands ached from handling so many memory-filled objects. His head throbbed with the echo of other people's grief. But they had moved everything that needed protection, reinforced the wards on the Archive door, and done everything they could to prevent another breach.

Warren locked the shop, and they stood outside on the sidewalk, staring at the building as if they could see all the memories inside. The sun had set, and Third Street was covered in twilight, making ordinary things look ominous.

"I'm losing this fight," Warren said quietly. "I've been losing for years, just trying to hold on until I could find someone to take over. But Vera is getting stronger, the wards are getting weaker, and I'm running out of time." He looked at Riley. "You need to learn faster than I expected. We have to speed up your training."

"How?"

Warren's face turned serious. "You need to experience more memories directly. You have to build up your tolerance and resistance. Right now, handling someone's trauma for a few minutes almost destroys you. But if you can learn to carry several memories at once and process pain without letting it overwhelm you, you'll be strong enough to keep the wards up when I'm gone."

Riley thought about Travis's memory, about how it had flooded his consciousness and left him barely functional for days. The idea of experiencing that multiplied, experiencing dozens or hundreds of memories at once, made his stomach turn. "That sounds like it would kill me."

"It might," Warren said. "But if you don't learn, and you can't handle the weight when I die, then everyone who trusted us will be at risk. Vera will take everything in the Archive, and Millbrook will see more deaths in a month than it has in a decade." He put a hand on Riley's shoulder. "I know it's not fair. I know you didn't ask for this. But you're all I have. You're all they have."

Riley looked up and down Third Street. A few people walked past—an elderly woman with groceries, a teenage kid on a skateboard, a young couple holding hands. Ordinary people living ordinary lives, unaware that their town sat on top of a convergence point where memories could be stored and entities could feed on pain. Unaware that Riley's choices in the next few weeks might determine whether they kept living or became Vera's next meal.

"Okay," Riley said. "Accelerate the training. Teach me how to carry the weight."

Warren nodded. "We start tomorrow. And Riley—prepare yourself. What you've experienced so far is nothing compared to what's coming."

Chapter Seven: The Immersion

Warren brought Riley into the Archive at dawn. The early light made the space look different. The shadows felt less menacing, and the shelves seemed more serious in a way, like a library built for suffering rather than knowledge. Riley's hands shook as he followed Warren to the center, where Warren had cleared a spot and drawn symbols on the floor with chalk.

"This is called an immersion," Warren said. "I'm going to lower your mental barriers and let you experience several memories at once. Your mind will want to sort them out one by one, but that's not the goal. You need to learn to hold them all together without letting one take over."

Riley looked at the chalk symbols. They reminded him of the wards on the Archive walls, but these seemed meant for opening up and making someone vulnerable, not for protection. "How many memories?"

"We'll start with three," Warren said. "Three separate traumas, each with a different emotional feel. If you can handle those, we'll add more. But Riley," Warren said, fixing his pale eyes on him, "this will be the hardest thing you've ever done." These memories will try to overwhelm you. They'll make you feel like their pain is your own, like their trauma is yours. You have to remember who you are. You're just the vessel, not the victim."

Riley wanted to back out. He wanted to say it was too much, too fast, and too risky. But he thought of Colleen's hollowed-out chest, Vera watching the shop for weak spots, and everyone who depended on this place to keep their worst memories safe. Like it or not, he had to stick with this.

"I'm ready," Riley said.

Warren gestured to the center of the chalk circle. "Lie down. Hands at your sides. Don't fight what's coming. Let it flow through you."

Riley lay down in the circle. The floor felt hard and cold against his back. The Archive's ceiling disappeared into shadows above him, and he felt as if he were lying at the bottom of a well, looking up at a distant opening.

Warren moved around the circle, touching specific symbols with his fingertips. Each symbol began to glow with that familiar silver light. "First memory," Warren said, and he placed a small object next to Riley's head. A child's toy car, red plastic worn smooth from years of handling. "This is Peter Jamison's. He brought the memory of his son's drowning. A family camping trip, a river moving faster than it looked, a seven-year-old boy who couldn't swim well enough."

The memory struck Riley hard. Suddenly, he was on a riverbank, watching a small boy struggle against the current. Panic rose in his chest—not his own, but Peter's. He felt the awful realization that he was too far away and couldn't reach his son in time. The water was cold and brown from recent rain, and it swallowed the boy in a moment. Riley dove in—no, Peter did—but the current was too strong and the river too deep. When he finally pulled his son to shore, the boy's lips were blue and his eyes were empty.

Riley gasped, his back arching off the floor. His lungs felt full of water even though he was breathing air. He could taste the river in his mouth, could feel the boy's cold skin beneath his hands.

"Second memory," Warren said, and he placed another object—a wedding ring. "This is Sheila Morrison's. Her husband's infidelity. Years of lying, gaslighting, making her feel crazy for suspecting the truth. The day she found the texts on his phone, the day her entire marriage revealed itself as a fiction."

The river memory stayed, replaying the drowning again and again as the second memory took hold. Now Riley was in a bedroom, holding a phone with shaking hands, reading message after message about another woman, another life, another side of the man she'd trusted for fifteen years. The betrayal felt like being gutted, like discovering reality itself had lied to her. This pain was different from the drowning—less sharp, more corrosive, the kind that eats away at someone slowly.

Riley tried to separate the memories and feel them one by one. But they stayed together, the drowning and the betrayal mixing, creating a wave of pain that made his whole body shake.

"Third memory," Warren said. His voice sounded distant now, coming from the other side of a thick wall. He placed a third object—a pill bottle. "This is Derek Foster's. His father's cancer. Months of watching a strong man waste away, of helping him to the bathroom because he was too weak to walk, of counting down morphine doses and pretending there was still hope."

The third memory hit Riley like a wave. Now he was sitting next to a hospital bed—no, a home hospice bed—watching his father struggle to breathe. The man's skin was yellow, his eyes sunken, his hands thin and bony. Riley could smell the scent of dying, sweet and rotten and chemical from the medicine. He heard the death rattle in his father's throat and felt helpless as someone he loved faded away in front of him.

Now, three memories played at once. The drowning boy. The betrayed wife. The dying father. Each one demanded all of Riley's attention, each insisting its pain was the only pain that mattered. Riley's mind split as he tried to hold them all, to be Peter, Sheila, and Derek at the same time, and to carry their suffering without breaking.

His body seized on the Archive floor. His hands clawed at the wooden boards, fingernails leaving scratches. Tears streamed down his face—whose tears? His own? The grieving father's? The betrayed wife's? He couldn't tell anymore where one person ended and another began.

"Hold them," Warren's voice commanded. "Don't let them consume you. Remember who you are. Riley Bennett. Twenty-two years old. College dropout. Your mother died of cancer. You're not these people. You're just carrying their pain temporarily."

But Riley couldn't remember who he was. He was Peter watching his son drown. He was Sheila reading those devastating texts. He was Derek holding his father's hand as the man took his last rattling breath. The memories filled every part of his mind, leaving no space for Riley's own identity.

Time lost all meaning. Riley was trapped in a place where all three traumas played on a loop: drowning, betrayal, and death. He was only faintly aware of his body on the Archive floor, Warren's hands on his forehead, and something being poured into his mouth that tasted like metal and earth.

Then, slowly, the memories began to separate.

Riley realized he could keep the drowning in one part of his mind while looking at the betrayal in another. He could feel Derek's grief without losing Peter's panic. The pain didn't get any less; each memory was still sharp and terrible. But Riley learned to make space between them, to compartmentalize, and to feel more than one trauma without losing himself.

Warren pulled Riley out of the circle. The older man's face looked drawn, aged, like he'd poured more of himself into keeping Riley alive than he could afford. "That's enough for today. You did it. Three memories held simultaneously. That's more than most keepers manage on their first immersion."

Riley couldn't speak. His throat was raw from screaming. When had he screamed? His whole body ached as if he'd run a marathon. But beneath the pain, he felt something else: a strange strength, a confidence that came from surviving something he thought would destroy him.

Warren helped Riley to his feet and guided him back to the front shop. Riley collapsed onto the stool behind the counter, his legs unable to support his weight. His hands shook uncontrollably, and his vision kept blurring at the edges.

"Drink this," Warren said, pressing a cup into Riley's hands. The liquid inside smelled like herbs and something mineral, like drinking from a mountain stream. Riley drank it anyway, and the shaking in his hands began to subside.

They sat in silence while Riley recovered. Outside the shop's windows, Millbrook went on with its Thursday morning: cars passing, people walking to work, the usual routines of a small town. But Riley felt cut off from that world now. He had touched something deeper, something more real than everyday life. He had held other people's worst moments in his mind and survived.

"How do you live with this?" Riley finally asked. "How do you hold hundreds of memories and not lose yourself completely?"

"You learn to build walls," Warren said. "Internal barriers that keep the memories from bleeding into your own thoughts. You learn which traumas can coexist and which ones need to be kept separate. And you learn to let them go when you're not actively storing them." He looked at Riley. "But I'll be honest—you never fully recover from an immersion. Each one leaves marks. Each one ages you in ways that aren't just physical."

Riley thought about Warren's prematurely gray hair, his weathered face, the way he moved like someone decades older than his actual years. "How many immersions have you done?"

"More than I can count. Hundreds, probably. Each time a memory comes in that's too dangerous to store normally, each time I need to re-inforce my ability to carry weight, I do another immersion." Warren's voice dropped. "It's killing me, Riley. Just like maintaining the wards is killing me. But it's necessary. Without these practices, the shop fails. The memories escape. The entities win."

Riley wanted to ask how Warren kept going, how he found the strength to pour himself into this building day after day knowing it would eventually kill him. But he already knew the answer. Warren kept going because people needed him. Because Millbrook sat on a convergence point where pain concentrated and memories could be stored, and someone had to guard that intersection between the phys-ical and emotional worlds.

"When's the next immersion?" Riley asked.

Warren looked surprised. "You want to do another one?"

"You said I need to learn fast. You said Vera's getting stronger and we're running out of time." Riley's hands had stopped shaking now. His vision had cleared. He felt hollowed out but functional, like a building that had been gutted and reinforced. "So let's not waste time.

Teach me everything you know. Use whatever methods work fastest. I can handle it."

Warren studied Riley's face for a long time. Then he smiled, and it was a real smile, warm and genuine. "You're going to make a good keeper, Riley Bennett. Better than me, probably. You've got something I never had: a willingness to sacrifice quickly instead of slowly bleeding out over years."

"I'm not sure that's a compliment," Riley said.

"It's not," Warren said. "But it's what this job needs. Fast sacrifice. Complete commitment. The willingness to burn bright instead of fade slowly." He stood up, walked to the window, and looked out at Third Street. "Tomorrow we'll do another immersion. Five memories this time. Then seven. Then ten. By next week, you should be able to hold twenty at once. By the end of the month, you'll be ready to maintain the wards yourself."

Riley felt the weight of that timeline settle onto his shoulders. A month to learn what usually took years. A month to become strong enough to protect hundreds of people's worst moments. A month before Warren died and Riley became the sole guardian of the Archive.

"What if I fail?" Riley asked quietly. "What if I'm not strong enough?" The possibility existed and Riley wanted some reassurance.

Warren turned from the window, and his pale eyes held something like faith. "You won't fail. I can see it in you—the same stubbornness that kept you alive after your mother died, that kept you working two jobs when you could have given up. You're a survivor, Riley. And survivors make the best keepers, because they know what's at stake."

Riley wanted to believe that. He wanted to believe he was strong enough for this impossible job. But he kept thinking about Colleen's hollowed-out chest, the four deaths in six months, and Vera watching the shop for weak spots. The task ahead felt too big, the enemies too strong, and the margin for error too small.

But he also remembered Brenda standing taller after letting go of her son's memory. He thought of Travis leaving the shop able to breathe again, and all the people who could keep living because someone guarded their pain for them.

"Alright," Riley said. "Tomorrow. Five memories. Let's do this."

Chapter Eight: The Breaking Point

The immersions became Riley's new reality. Every morning he lay down in Warren's chalk circle while the older man placed objects around him: wedding rings, photographs, children's toys, medication bottles. Each one was an anchor to someone's worst day. The memories rushed into Riley's mind in waves, piling up until he thought his brain might break from the strain.

Five memories. Then seven. Then ten. Each immersion pushed Riley closer to his limit, but each one also taught him how to carry more, how to separate the pain, and how to hold onto himself while feeling so many others' suffering.

By the third week, Riley could handle twenty memories at once. He had learned to move between experiences, feeling Peter's grief for his drowned son while also carrying Sheila's betrayal, Derek's helplessness, and many other traumas. His body changed too: he lost weight even though he ate more, his eyes had dark circles, and his hands shook unless he was holding memory objects.

Warren looked worse. The older man had aged years in weeks, his face now almost skeletal, his movements slow and painful. Each time he maintained the wards, he gave more of himself than he could afford, and the building demanded more and more frequent renewals as Vera pressed harder against the barriers.

Riley realized they were both dying. Warren was fading quickly, Riley more slowly. The shop was draining them, using their life to protect the memories. Neither could stop, because if they did, everyone else would be in danger sooner.

On a Tuesday morning in Riley's fourth week at the shop, everything came undone.

Riley was handling a transaction—a woman named Vicki who wanted to store the memory of her miscarriage—when he felt the wards shudder. The sensation rolled through the building like an earthquake, making the guitars swing on their hooks and the jewelry rattle in its case. Warren's face went pale.

"She's here," Warren said. "Vera. She's found a way through."

The temperature plummeted. Frost spread across the windows so fast it made crackling sounds. The lights flickered and dimmed, leaving the shop in twilight gloom. Riley could feel something pressing against the building from the outside, something massive and hungry and absolutely furious.

Vicki screamed. She stumbled backward, away from the counter, her eyes wide with terror at something Riley couldn't yet see. "What is that? What the hell is that?"

Riley saw her then. Vera appeared in the corner of the shop, but not in her old, almost human form. This time she was a shadow with too many edges, a darkness that moved strangely, a shape that was painful to look at. Only her colorless eyes looked human, and they locked onto Warren with a hungry stare.

"Your wards are broken," Vera said. Her voice came from everywhere at once, layered and terrible. "Forty years I've waited, forty years I've circled this building waiting for you to weaken enough. And now I can finally feed."

Warren moved between Vera and the Archive door. His body was frail, diminished, but he stood firm. "You're not getting in. I'll burn what's left of my life maintaining the inner wards. I'll turn myself into the barrier."

"You'll die for nothing," Vera said. "I've already consumed four of your clients. Their memories were delicious, but they were just appetizers. The Archive contains centuries of concentrated pain, of refined trauma. I'll feast for decades on what you've collected."

Riley felt the memories in the Archive reaching out, reacting to Vera's presence. They wanted to be consumed, to be freed from storage even if it meant being destroyed. The building was failing, its protections breaking down, its structure weakening under Vera's attack.

Vicki bolted for the door. She got it open and ran out into Third Street, leaving Riley and Warren alone with Vera.

"Riley," Warren said, his voice steady despite his fear, "get everyone out. Use the emergency protocol—call everyone who's stored a memory here and tell them to leave Millbrook. Get as far away as possible. When the Archive falls, the memories will return to their owners corrupted. They need to be somewhere they can get help, somewhere with hospitals and crisis centers."

"I'm not leaving you," Riley said.

"You don't have a choice." Warren pulled something from his pocket: a small, ceremonial-looking knife with symbols carved into its handle. "This is the keeper's final option. I can bind my life force directly into the wards, make myself part of the building's protection. It'll buy you time to evacuate the clients, to get them somewhere safe. Then you run too."

"No," Riley said. The word came out stronger than he felt. "There has to be another way. We can fight her together, we can—"

"There is no together," Warren interrupted. His pale eyes met Riley's, and Riley saw absolute certainty there. "I'm dying anyway. Have been for months. The immersions, the ward maintenance, forty years of carrying weight have all caught up with me. I have maybe days left. But if I do this, if I bind myself now, I can give you weeks. Enough time to find another solution, to get the clients to safety, to maybe, maybe save some of what we've built here."

Vera laughed, and the sound was like glass breaking. "How noble. The old keeper sacrificing himself for the lost cause. It won't matter, Warren. Even if you bind yourself, I'll just wait. I'm patient. I've existed for centuries. I can wait a few more weeks."

Warren looked at Riley one last time. "There's a ledger behind the counter. Lists every client, every memory, every contact number. Get them out. And Riley—don't try to be a keeper. Don't try to maintain this shop. Let it fall. Some things aren't meant to be saved."

Before Riley could respond, Warren plunged the ceremonial knife into his own chest.

Blood spread across Warren's shirt, dark and sudden. But instead of collapsing, Warren stood straighter. The symbols on the knife started to glow, and that light moved through Warren's body, lighting him up from the inside like a lantern. He turned to the Archive door and pressed both hands against it.

The binding happened quickly. Warren's body faded, turning translucent, then transparent, and finally disappearing into the wood of the door. The symbols Riley had seen on the walls appeared on

Warren's skin as he vanished, silver light pulsing with a heartbeat that slowed and then stopped.

And then Warren was gone. He wasn't dead; Riley could still feel him, his presence woven into the building itself, but he was no longer human. Warren had become part of the shop's structure and protection, a guardian bound forever to the place he had defended for forty years.

Riley couldn't breathe. He stood frozen, staring at the Archive door where Warren had vanished, unable to process what he'd just witnessed. The older man had been teaching him, guiding him, preparing him to take over, and now he was gone. Not dead but not alive either. Trapped between states, sacrificed to buy time for an evacuation Riley didn't even know how to coordinate.

Vera hissed. Her shadow form pressed harder against the shop's boundaries, testing the new wards and searching for weaknesses. But Warren's binding held. The Archive door glowed with silver light, symbols flickering across its surface, and Vera couldn't get through.

"Clever," Vera said. Her colorless eyes fixed on Riley. "But temporary. He's given you what—three weeks? A month? Then his life force burns out completely, the binding fails, and I get everything. What will you do with that time, little keeper? Run? Watch from a distance as I consume centuries of stored pain?"

Riley's hands clenched into fists. His whole body shook with grief, rage, and the weight of twenty memories still swirling in his mind from that morning's immersion. He looked at Vera's shadow form, saw the hunger coming off her like heat, and made a decision.

"No," Riley said. "I'm going to stop you."

Vera laughed again. "How? You're barely trained. You can't maintain the wards without burning yourself out in weeks like Warren did. You can't fight me directly. I'll consume you the moment you step outside this building's protections. You're a college dropout with debt problems who stumbled into a job he doesn't understand. You're nothing."

Riley thought about his mother's hospital room. He remembered the medical bills that haunted him. He thought about dropping out of college because he couldn't afford both tuition and grief. He remembered every time someone told him he wasn't enough, wasn't smart enough, wasn't strong enough, wasn't anything enough.

Then he thought about Brenda, who stood taller after letting go of her son's memory. He thought about Travis, who breathed easier after storing his survivor's guilt. He remembered Colleen and the three others who died because keepers failed. He thought about Warren binding himself to the building to give Riley time he didn't deserve.

"You're right," Riley said. "I don't know what I'm doing. I'm scared and overwhelmed and completely unprepared for this. But I'm also stubborn. And I'm tired of entities like you deciding who gets to carry pain and who gets consumed by it. So here's what's going to happen: I'm going to learn everything Warren didn't have time to teach me. I'm going to find a way to reinforce these wards permanently. And I'm going to turn this shop into a fortress you can never break through."

"Impossible," Vera said.

"Maybe," Riley said. "But I'm going to try anyway. And while I do, I'll get every client somewhere safe. I'll make sure that if this shop falls, if it does, there's no one left for you to hurt."

Vera's shadow-form rippled with what might have been frustration. "Warren was right about one thing. You're a survivor. Survivors are annoying. They keep fighting long after most people would quit." Her colorless eyes narrowed. "Fine. Three weeks, Riley Bennett. That's how long Warren's binding will last. After that, I'm coming in, and nothing you do will matter." Only the smell of ozone and the lingering cold remained.

Riley stood alone in the shop. Or not truly alone—he could feel Warren woven into the building, sense the older man's presence like a hand on his shoulder. He looked around at all the anchors to other people's pain: the guitars, the jewelry, the sports equipment, and the hundreds of objects in the Archive. Each one was someone's trust, someone's hope, someone's desperate attempt to keep living despite unbearable memories.

Warren had told him to let the shop fail, to evacuate the clients and run. But Riley couldn't do it. He wouldn't. If the shop fell and Vera got into the Archive, everyone who trusted the keepers would be destroyed. The next place where memories could be stored would be at risk too.

Riley moved behind the counter and found the ledger Warren had mentioned. It was old, leather-bound, with pages filled with names and addresses and phone numbers written in careful handwriting that had changed subtly over forty years. Hundreds of clients. Hundreds of people depending on this building to keep them safe.

Riley flipped to the back of the ledger and found blank pages. He picked up Warren's pen and began to write.

Day One After Warren's Binding: I need to learn how to maintain the wards on my own. I need to find a way to strengthen the protections without giving up my life force. I need to contact the clients and warn them about the danger. I need to figure out how to fight an entity that's been hunting for centuries.

I don't know if I can do this. But I have to try.

Riley closed the ledger and looked at the Archive door. The symbols still glowed silver, pulsing with Warren's bound life force. The older man had given everything to buy time, to give Riley a chance at finding a solution.

Riley wouldn't waste that chance. He couldn't. Too many people depended on him now.

Chapter Nine: The Convergence

Three weeks went by in a rush of frantic research and failed experiments. Riley used every moment to search for a way to strengthen the wards without risking his own life like Warren had. He contacted every client from Warren's records, warning them about the danger. He told them to leave Millbrook if possible, or at least be ready for their memories to come back changed if the shop fell.

Some listened, but most didn't. They had given their pain to the Memory Keeper and believed, or wanted to believe, that the shop would last forever.

Riley knew the truth. He felt Warren's life force grow weaker each day, saw the symbols on the Archive door fade, and sensed Vera drawing nearer as the protections weakened. The three-week deadline was almost here, and Riley still hadn't found a way to save the shop.

On the last night, Riley sat alone in the Archive, surrounded by hundreds of stored memories. Earlier, he had tried another immersion, hoping that holding enough memories at once might help him find a way to fight Vera. Instead, he only proved what he already knew: he was not strong enough. He could manage twenty memories, maybe thirty on a good day. But to keep the wards up for good, to become the building's guardian like Warren, Riley would have to carry hundreds, maybe even thousands.

It would kill him. It would burn him out in weeks, just as it had done to Warren.

But what choice did he have?

Riley put his hands on the Archive floor and let his mind sink into the building's foundation. He could sense Warren there, more memory than man now, his awareness faded to almost nothing. Warren had given everything, and soon all that would remain of him would be another memory of sacrifice.

"I don't know how to save this place," Riley whispered into the empty Archive. "I don't know how to fight her. I'm sorry, Warren. I'm sorry I'm not enough."

The Archive stayed silent. But Riley sensed a change in the air, a shift in pressure that made his ears pop. He looked up and saw her.

Vera stood at the Archive's entrance, her shadowy form spreading darkness across the floor. She was not alone. Behind her, Riley saw other entities—shapes that were painful to look at, hungers given form, all the things that fed on human pain gathered together. They had waited for this moment, for the wards to fall, for a chance to reach centuries of stored trauma.

"It's time," Vera said. Her colorless eyes gleamed with anticipation. "Warren's binding has failed. The Archive is open. And you're standing between us and the greatest feast we've encountered in decades."

Riley stood up. His legs shook, but he stayed on his feet. He thought about running, about escaping through a back door if there was one, about saving himself and letting Millbrook's convergence point fall to the entities that would destroy everything.

Then he remembered Brenda's face when she left the shop, standing taller. He thought of Travis breathing easier. He thought of his mother in her hospital bed, carrying pain no one could take from her, dying without the choice Riley had given to others.

"No," Riley said. "You're not getting these memories. You're not consuming anyone else."

"How will you stop us?" Vera asked. "You can't keep the wards up. You can't fight us. You're just one tired keeper facing an army of hungry entities. What can you possibly do?"

Riley looked around the Archive at all the stored memories. There were hundreds, maybe thousands, each one a moment of pain someone had been able to let go of, but not carry alone. There were memories of drowning children, betrayed spouses, dying parents. Memories of abuse, loss, regret, and grief. So much suffering, so much trauma, all kept safe in this strange place.

Then Riley realized something. The memories were not just stored here—they were protected. Not only by the wards, but by the building itself, by the convergence point below, and by the generations of keepers who had given themselves to this place. The Archive wanted to keep these moments safe.

Riley just needed to help it.

He knelt and put both hands flat on the Archive floor. Then he opened himself up fully—not just to three or five or twenty memories, but to all of them. Every stored moment in the building rushed into Riley's mind at once.

The pain was immediate and absolute. Riley felt himself drowning, felt himself being betrayed, felt himself dying of cancer and overdosing on heroin and losing children and watching parents fade. He experienced every trauma stored in the Archive all at once, and his mind shattered under the weight.

But under all that pain, something else happened. The memories recognized Riley as a keeper, someone trying to protect them. Instead of crushing him, they started to organize themselves. They formed a network, a web of shared pain that Riley could use without being destroyed. Each memory supported the others, spreading out the weight and making it possible to carry pain that would break any one person.

Riley stood up. His body moved strangely, jerky and uncoordinated, like a puppet with tangled strings. Blood ran from his nose, ears, and the corners of his eyes. His breath came in ragged gasps. But he was standing, carrying every memory in the Archive, and now he understood how Warren had lasted forty years.

You didn't carry the weight alone. You let the memories carry each other.

Riley looked at Vera and the entities behind her. His voice came out layered, speaking with the voices of hundreds of people whose pain he now carried. "These memories belong to people who trusted us. They gave us their worst moments because they believed someone would keep them safe. And I'm going to honor that trust."

He pressed his hands into the Archive floor. Not literally—his hands stayed on the surface—but his mind plunged deep, down to the convergence point under the building, to the place where the barrier between the physical and emotional worlds was thinnest.

And Riley bound himself to it.

He didn't do it the way Warren had, by tying his life force to the wards. Instead, Riley bound his mind to the convergence point itself, making himself part of the place, becoming a permanent part of where memories could be kept. He felt his body dissolve, felt himself spread through the building's foundation, and felt his awareness grow to cover the whole shop, the Archive, and all the memories inside.

The pain was endless. Riley felt himself dying, drowning, being betrayed, and losing everyone all at once, feeling every trauma at full strength with nothing to block them. But he held on. He let the memories flow through him instead of into him. He became a channel instead of an endpoint.

New wards appeared on the Archive walls. They weren't silver symbols carved into wood, but shapes made from Riley's own mind, woven into the building's structure. They glowed with power drawn not from a keeper's life, but from the convergence point itself, from the place itself.

Vera screamed. The other entities scattered, unable to approach the reinforced protections. The Archive door slammed shut, sealing itself with Riley's awareness. And the shop transformed into something more than a building—it became a living ward, a guardian entity in itself, powered by Riley's consciousness and the convergence point's energy and the collective strength of every memory stored within.

Riley was no longer fully human. He existed partly in the physical world and partly in the emotional realm, stretched thin across both. He was aware of every person in Millbrook who carried pain. He could feel their suffering, sense when someone needed to bring a memory to the shop, and protect stored moments without asking anyone to give up their life to keep the wards.

But he had lost something too. His body was gone, dissolved into the building's foundation. His human life was over. He could not leave the shop, could not touch anything physical, and could not exist as Riley Bennett anymore.

He had become the Memory Keeper in the truest sense, bound forever to his post, unable to live or die, both cursed and blessed to guard the pain of others for all time.

Chapter Ten: The New Keeper

Six months after Riley's transformation, Brenda returned to the shop.

She walked through the door with a new confidence Riley hadn't seen before. Her posture was straighter and she moved with an ease that suggested she had learned to breathe freely again. She glanced around the familiar shop with a small smile, then spoke to what looked like empty air.

"Riley? Are you here?"

Riley appeared in front of the counter. He no longer had a physical body, but his consciousness took a shape that still looked like him. His form was see-through and flickered at the edges, showing that he was only partly present in the physical world.

"I'm here," Riley said. His voice sounded normal, which was good. He'd been practicing.

Brenda's smile grew. "I heard what happened. The whole town is talking about it. They say the shop wouldn't fall, and the keeper became the building. Some people call you a ghost. Others say you're a guardian spirit. No one really knows what to call you."

"I barely know what to call myself," Riley admitted. He gestured around the shop. "But I'm keeping the memories safe. That's what matters."

"I wanted to thank you," Brenda said. "And to bring you something." She reached into her bag and pulled out a photograph. It showed a young boy with a gap-toothed smile, holding a baseball glove. Kevin. "I can remember the good parts now. His laugh, his energy, how much he loved playing catch. I couldn't access those memories before because the bad one was blocking everything. But now... now I can hold both. The grief and the joy."

Riley felt something warm spread through his consciousness. This was why he'd done it. Why he'd sacrificed his body, his human life, his chance at normal existence. So people like Brenda could heal, could remember their loved ones without being destroyed by the memories.

In the months that followed, news about the new Memory Keeper spread through Millbrook and beyond. People came from nearby towns and even from across the state, bringing their hardest memories and trusting Riley to keep them safe. The shop grew in ways that seemed impossible, the Archive getting bigger as more memories arrived. Riley's awareness grew too, learning to carry pain in ways Warren had never thought possible.

Travis visited on Thursdays. He'd sit in the shop for an hour, not always talking, just existing in a space where someone understood what he'd experienced. Sometimes he'd ask Riley questions about Mitchell, about carrying guilt, about surviving when others didn't. Riley couldn't provide easy answers, but he could listen with the authority of someone who'd carried Travis's worst memory directly.

More people arrived. More memories were stored. Riley learned to sense when someone in Millbrook was close to being overwhelmed by pain, and he would send a gentle nudge, a feeling or an impulse, toward the shop. Sometimes they came. Sometimes they didn't. Riley could only offer help, not force it.

Vera never came back. The other entities that fed on pain now avoided the shop, sensing that something important had changed and that this place was now protected. Sometimes Riley sensed them at the edge of town, searching for people who were vulnerable or in pain. When that happened, he would reach out and gently guide those people toward help, whether it was a therapist, a hospital, or any resource that could keep them safe until they could come to the shop.

He saved some. Lost others. Learned to carry the grief of his failures alongside all the other pain stored in the Archive.

One night, though Riley wasn't sure if it was truly night or just felt that way, he sensed Warren's presence stir. The older man had been silent since his binding, his awareness faded to almost nothing. But now he managed a few words, sending his thoughts straight into Riley's mind.

"You did it. You found a way I never imagined."

"I'm not sure this counts as success," Riley responded. "I'm not human anymore. I can't leave. I'll exist like this until the convergence point fails or the building falls or the world ends."

"But the memories are safe. The people are safe. That's what mattered."

Riley thought about that. He existed in a state that was barely alive, carrying hundreds of people's worst moments, unable to touch physical objects or eat or sleep or do any of the things that made human life bearable. But he also existed in a state where he could protect trauma from being weaponized, where he could keep people from drowning in their own pain, where he could be useful in a way he'd never been as a struggling college dropout.

"Yeah," Riley said. "I guess it is."

Warren's presence faded into silence again, and Riley turned his focus back to the shop. Outside the windows, Third Street kept its usual pace. People walked by, cars passed, and life went on with all its joys and pains. Riley could sense everyone on that street, feel the memories they carried, and sometimes know who needed help before they did.

A young woman paused outside the shop's door. She stood there for a long time, staring at the sign in the window: MEMORY KEEP-ER. SERIOUS INQUIRIES ONLY. Her hand reached for the door-knob, hesitated, withdrew. She was afraid. Afraid of judgment, afraid of appearing weak, afraid that giving up a memory would make her less herself.

Riley sent her a gentle thought: It's okay to need help. It's okay to let go of a burden you were never meant to carry alone.

The woman pushed open the door.

Riley appeared behind the counter, trying to look as welcoming as possible. "Hi," he said. "What are you carrying?"

And the woman began to speak, and Riley began to listen, and the work continued.

That was what keepers did. They listened, carried, and protected. They helped others keep living, even when life felt impossible.

Riley Bennett might not be human anymore, but now he was truly doing something that mattered.

Author's Note: "The Memory Keeper's Apprentice" is the first in a planned series exploring Riley's work protecting Millbrook's convergence point and the various memories that pass through his shop. Future novellas will delve deeper into the nature of emotional trauma, the entities that feed on pain, and what it means to carry suffering on behalf of others.

About the Author

P. A. Farrell is an accomplished flash fiction author whose compelling micro-narratives have captivated readers across the literary landscape. With over forty publications in prestigious online journals and literary magazines, Farrell has established herself as a master of the abbreviated form, crafting complete worlds and complex emotions within the constraints of brief word counts.

Her expertise in flash fiction extends beyond individual pieces to comprehensive collections, where she shows remarkable range and consistency in delivering powerful, bite-sized stories that linger long after the last sentence. Each collection showcases her ability to explore diverse themes, characters, and settings while maintaining the precision and impact that define exceptional flash fiction.

Farrell's work resonates with readers who appreciate literature that delivers maximum emotional and intellectual impact in minimal space. Her stories often examine the pivotal moments that define the human experience, capturing the essence of larger truths through carefully chosen details and expertly crafted prose. The breadth of her publication history speaks both to her prolific output and the consistent quality that editors and readers expect from her work.

Through her continued contributions to the flash fiction genre, P.A. Farrell has become a trusted voice for readers seeking literature that respects their time while enriching their understanding of the human condition. Her collections offer the perfect opportunity to experience the full range of her storytelling abilities in a single, cohesive volume.

In her other life, P. A. Farrell is a clinical psychologist who has written several self-help books and continues to contribute to media outlets such as Medium.com and Butterfly, where she posts articles on all aspects of healthcare, mental health, and a variety of other topics. Her Author's Page is here: https://tinyurl.com/4ewdunb8

Books by P. A. Farrell

Snowbound Hearts
   The Secrets We Keep
   The Secrets We Keep 2
   Whispers Across the Sea
   Love by the Latte
   Echoes of Expectation—Waiting
   Unexpected Short Tales of Surprise

A Special Request

If this book has touched your heart, sparked your curiosity, or simply entertained you along the way, I'd be incredibly grateful if you could take a moment to share your thoughts with a review on Amazon or wherever you discovered this book. Your words not only help other readers find books they'll love, but they also mean the world to authors like me who pour their hearts into every page. Thank you for being part of this journey, and for helping stories find their way to the readers who need them most. Her Author Page on Amazon: https://tinyurl.com/4ewdunb8

www.ingramcontent.com/pod-product-compliance
Lightning Source LLC
Chambersburg PA
CBHW030529260626
47157CB00005B/1945